Roseanne Greenfield

NOO

MAC

Orchard Books · New York · An Imprint of Scholastic Inc.

Thong   illustrated by Meilo So

To Maya, who creates magic with her ideas — *R.G.T.*

All things simple — *M.S.*

Text copyright © 2014 by Roseanne Greenfield Thong
Illustrations copyright © 2014 by Meilo So

Library of Congress Cataloging-in-Publication Data
Thong, Roseanne, author. Noodle magic / Roseanne Greenfield Thong ; Meilo So. —First edition.
pages cm
Summary: Grandpa Tu is famous
for his special noodles, and as the emperor's
birthday approaches, he encourages his
granddaughter, Mei, to find her own noodle magic.
ISBN 978-0-545-52167-3
1. Noodles—Juvenile fiction. 2. Holiday
cooking—Juvenile fiction. 3. Magic—
Juvenile fiction. 4. Grandparent and
child—Juvenile fiction. 5. Grandfathers—
Juvenile fiction. 6. Granddaughters—
Juvenile fiction. [1. Noodles—Fiction.
2. Cooking—Fiction. 3. Magic—Fiction.
4. Grandfathers—Fiction. 5. China—History—
Fiction.] I. So, Meilo, illustrator. II. Title.
PZ7.T3815No 2014
813.6—dc23   2014000006
10 9 8 7 6 5 4 3 2 1   14 15 16 17 18
Printed in Malaysia 108
First edition, December 2014
The text type was set in Avenir LT. The display type was set
in Post Mediaeval and Bitstream Chianti BT Italic Swash.
Book design by Chelsea C. Donaldson

The emperor's birthday was coming, and excitement filled the air.

Every day, Mei watched Grandpa Tu make magic with his hands and a bit of dough. She loved the powdery flakes that hung in the air and freckled the morning light.

Every evening, Grandpa SLAPPED the dough on the table,
kneaded it with his hands, and stretched it into coils.
Everyone oohed and aahed over Grandpa Tu's noodles —
even the Moon Goddess, who brightened the night sky.

"Can you make a jump rope from noodles?" asked Mei.

"Simple as a sunflower seed," said Grandpa.

"How about string for our kites?" a neighbor asked.

"Easy as a sea breeze," said Grandpa.

Late that night, as the Moon Goddess lit up the sky, Mei heard SLAP, *knead*, stretch.

The next morning, Mei and her friends played and jumped

with strands of white, wheaty dough. "If only I had your gift," Mei sighed.

"I think you just might," said Grandpa.

But Mei knew that no one could spin magic like Grandpa Tu!

One afternoon, Mei watched the sky fill with fluffy, pink creatures. "Can you catch clouds with noodles?" she asked. "Fast as a flying fish," said Grandpa.

That night, as moonlight flooded the room, Mei watched Grandpa SLAP, *knead*, and `stretch`. The next morning, they gathered streams of fluffy, pink clouds just as the sun was rising.

"Your magic's the best," said Mei.

"But it's time for *you* to learn," Grandpa said.

On the day before the emperor's birthday, everyone was making something special — everyone except for Grandpa Tu.

The villagers were puzzled. Noodles were needed on every table — especially long-life noodles for the emperor.

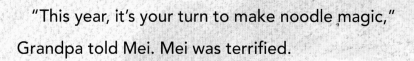

"This year, it's your turn to make noodle magic," Grandpa told Mei. Mei was terrified.

She measured carefully, and together they SLAPPED, *kneaded*, and stretched. "The rest is up to you," Grandpa said.

But as hard as she tried, Mei's noodles were as ordinary as a pot of white rice. She had to think of something, quick!

"Can *you* give me magic?" she asked Grandpa.

Grandpa stroked his beard. "Trust in yourself, Mei," he said.

Mei doubted Grandpa. She had never made noodle magic before!

The moon shone brightly into the workroom as Mei thought hard.

"Can noodles reach the moon?" she asked.

"That's as wishful as the wind." Grandpa laughed. "Whatever for?"

"A gift for the Moon Goddess," said Mei. "I could ask *her* for magic in return."

"You have all the magic you need!" said Grandpa Tu.

That night as Grandpa slept, Mei tried to SLAP and *knead.*

Just before sunrise, Grandpa returned.

"My hands are tired," said Mei.
"My arms aren't strong enough.
Can you help?"
  Grandpa nodded.

Together, they **stretched** and **pulled**,
until her dough reached the forest's edge.

Mei spun the dough into a huge ball of noodles and tossed it skyward. Faster and faster, it spiraled into space. As it got close to the moon, she watched it shrink to the size of a wheel, then a pumpkin, and finally, a tiny dot.

Mei called out to the Moon Goddess. "The village needs noodles for the emperor's birthday. I need some of your magic."

The Moon Goddess was delighted with
the gift, though she knew Mei had
to do this job herself.

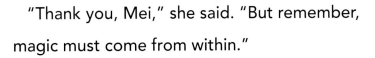

"Thank you, Mei," she said. "But remember, magic must come from within."

Mei took a deep breath. She *had* to think of something. She closed her eyes tight and remembered all that Grandpa Tu had shown her.

With a tug-of-war twang, Mei yanked her end of the noodles.

They stretched back and forth, up and down, until finally,

there was a SNAP!

The sky rained noodles. Small bow ties and pillows. Large coils and springs. It was a meteor shower of dough! There was enough for everyone's celebration — including a magical long-life strand for the emperor.

Mei's noodles *had* turned to magic. It was inside her all along!

From then on, the only sounds in Mei's workshop were

SLAP, *knead*, stretch, and . . .

WHOA!